LIZZY'S Ups and Downs

Not An Ordinary School Day

By Jessica Harper
Illustrated by
Lindsay Harper duPont

HarperCollinsPublishers

Special thanks to George Harper duPont

Lizzy's Ups and Downs: *Not an Ordinary School Day* • Text copyright © 2004 by Jessica Harper • Illustrations copyright © 2004 by Lindsay Harper duPont • Manufactured in China by South China Printing Company Ltd. All rights reserved. • www.harperchildrens.com • Library of Congress Cataloging-in-Publication Data • Harper, Jessica. Lizzy's ups and downs : not an ordinary school day / by Jessica Harper ; illustrated by Lindsay Harper duPont. — 1st ed. p. cm. Summary: Lizzy tells her mother all about her up and down feelings at school that day. ISBN 0-06-052063-9 — ISBN 0-06-052064-7 (lib. bdg.) [1. Emotions—Fiction. 2. Schools—Fiction. 3. Stories in rhyme.] I. Dupont, Lindsay Harper, ill. II. Title. PZ8.3.H219Lk 2004 [E]—dc21 2003009564 • Typography by Stephanie Bart-Horvath 2 3 4 5 6 7 8 9 10 • ❖ • First Edition

For Tommy, Elizabeth, and Nora,
whom I love with all their ups and downs
—J.H.

For Maya, Zubin, Sophie, and Iris
—L.H.dP.

"So, Lizzy," said her mom, "

Okay, so you remember that I slept late, so I hurried?

I thought that I might miss the bus—
that always makes me WORRIED.
I rushed to put my rain boots on
and brush my messy hair,

and (phew!) I made the bus,
but you know that 'cause you were there.

I wanted to sit next to Claire
since it was her last day,
because tomorrow she is moving
very far away.
But that boy Ray—he's such a pest—
he sat next to her first
and started singing "Row Your Boat"
so loud your ears could burst!

I felt so FRUSTRATED!
Ray thinks he's such a riot.
The driver finally shouted,
"Can we have some peace and quiet?"

At school I got EMBARRASSED,
'cause my left sock was white,
but by mistake
I'd put my Halloween sock on my right!

Claire said, "No one will notice."
She's really very sweet.
Of course, Ray took one look and said,
"Hey, Lizzy, TRICK OR TREAT!"

In science class we learned a song
about the stegosaurus.
We got through all the verses and were
working on the chorus
when Ray reached in his pocket and
pulled out a big green snake!
I screamed and dropped my music book.
He laughed and said, "It's fake!"

So then I went from being SCARED
to being really MAD!
When Ray went to the principal,
I secretly felt GLAD.

Ruby has a new lunch box—
it's shaped like a TV.
It sort of made me JEALOUS.
I'd like one like that for me.

I felt GOOD, because
I had those chocolate coins to share.
And Ruby split her string cheese,
and Claire brought Gummi Bears.

Then Mrs. Fox said I could read
my nature poem out loud.
I was pretty NERVOUS—
but they clapped, so I felt PROUD.

baloon   joke   pickel

circus   laff   popcorn

fair   princess

feest   ine

gorilla   hamster

jump   funny

ri   splash

h   vheel

But I was sooooo DISAPPOINTED. . . .
On the Friday spelling test,
I got four wrong. "Balloon" and "laugh"
and . . . I forget the rest.

Math was fun.
We did addition, using jelly beans.
I had six pinks and then I had to
add them to eight greens.

I was so ANNOYED, 'cause
I could swear Ray ate a ton.
He added ten reds to nine blues
and ended up with one!

Then it was time to go.
"Three cheers for Claire!" said Mrs. Fox.
It made me feel so SAD to watch
Claire pack her pencil box.
I gave her my eraser,
the one shaped like a whale.
She said she'd send me photos
of her new house in the mail.
Ruby gave her stationery.
Claire tried not to cry.

Her mother came. I'll miss her.
The whole class waved good-bye.

Our bus was kind of late, and,
in the rain, we stood and waited.
My new umbrella broke,
so I was very IRRITATED!
I took a seat with Ruby,
and Ray sat in front of us.
For once he didn't talk too much.
It was a quiet bus.

But when Ray's on a bus, well,
you just know there will be trouble.
He chewed a wad of bubble gum
and blew a giant bubble!
Everyone was giggling
and Ray just kept on blowing.
When we got off at Ruby's house,
his bubble was still growing!

I was SURPRISED when Ruby said,
"Ray's not so awful, is he?"
He did seem nicer. Maybe it was
'cause his mouth was busy!

We ate sugar popcorn
and we played a game of Twister.
We got really SILLY,
'til we thought of Claire and missed her.

I'm HAPPY to be home
after a crazy day like this,
just giving Joe a big fat hug
and Millicent a kiss!

Oh, what a day!

"Does this whole world have

ups and downs like mine?"

"Sometimes. And how do you feel now?"
"Oh, Mama, I feel FINE!"